# The Secret Life of SQUIRRELS

## A L♥VE STORY

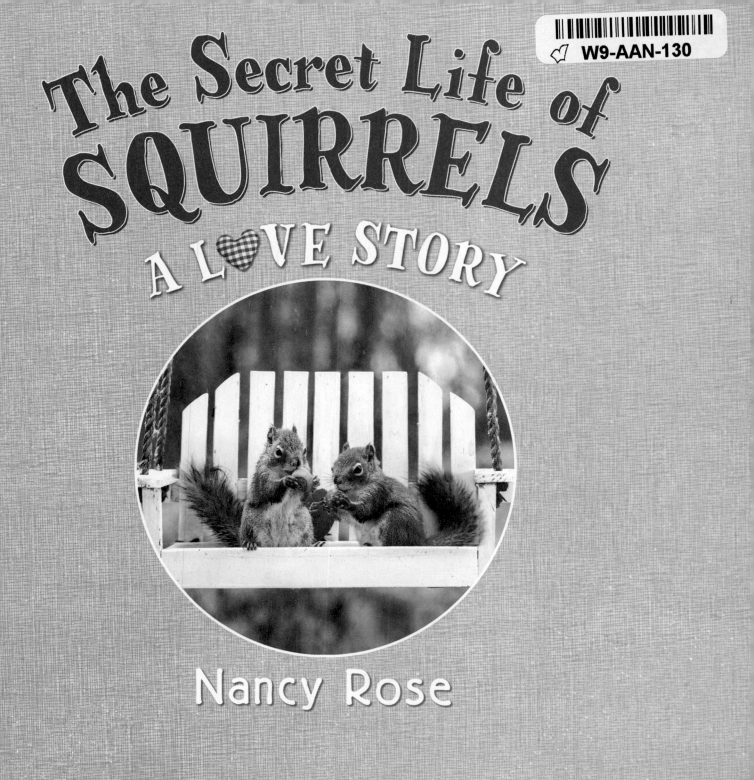

## Nancy Rose

SCHOLASTIC INC.

**M**ost squirrels spend their
days scrambling up trees
and searching for nuts.
Not Mr. Peanuts!
He is a rather unusual squirrel.

Valentine's Day is coming soon. Mr. Peanuts enjoys decorating for the holiday. Nice job, Mr. Peanuts!

But Valentine's Day can also be lonely, and Mr. Peanuts wishes he could meet another unusual squirrel to celebrate with. Mr. Peanuts tries to distract himself by working in his shed. But he can only think about how he would like to have someone to build something for.

Shopping for food would be more fun
if he were cooking dinner for a friend.

Mr. Peanuts goes to the park, but he doesn't have a friend to play with.

Mr. Peanuts is sad.
Being the only squirrel
like him can be hard
sometimes.
Please don't cry,
Mr. Peanuts!

On the way home, Mr. Peanuts stops
at the neighborhood wishing well.
Usually, Mr. Peanuts wishes for more
acorns, but today he wants to wish
for someone special.

Whenever Mr. Peanuts is feeling especially lonely, he goes to the bookstore. That always cheers him up.

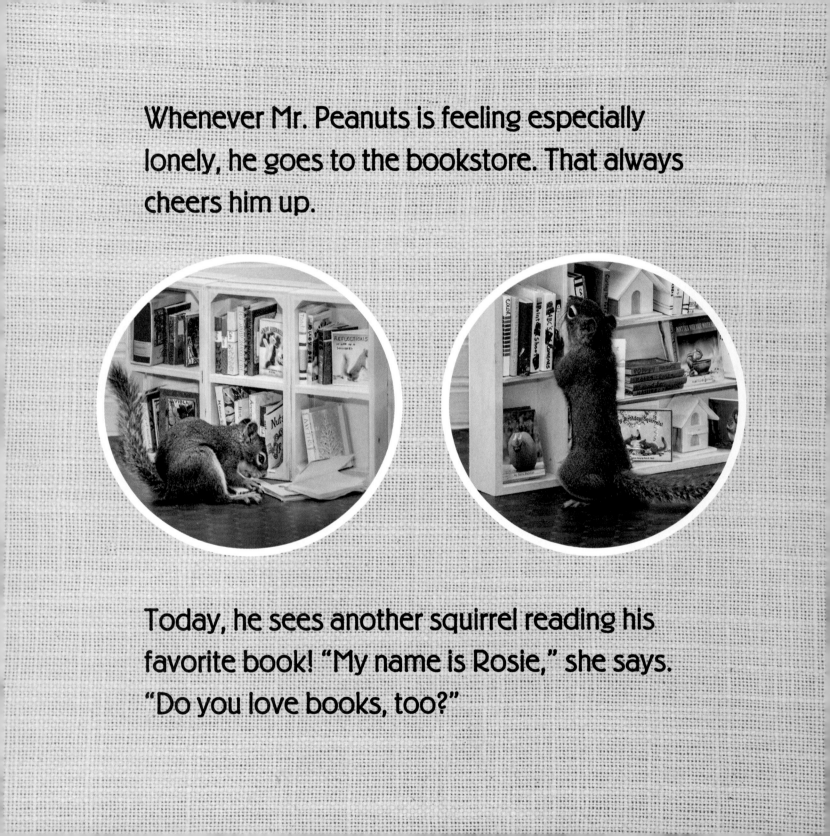

Today, he sees another squirrel reading his favorite book! "My name is Rosie," she says. "Do you love books, too?"

After they leave the bookstore, Mr. Peanuts and Rosie begin chattering about books...
and sunflower seeds. Finally, Mr. Peanuts has a special squirrel friend!

Mr. Peanuts and Rosie go to the park to play hopscotch with their peanuts. (It's easy to hop when you have four legs.)

No, Rosie, that nut
is for *playing*, not *eating*!

Squirrels are used to climbing trees,
so climbing a swing set is easy!

Mr. Peanuts decides to show
Rosie his favorite game:
jumping from trees!
Look at Mr. Peanuts go!

As the sun goes down,
Mr. Peanuts realizes he's
absolutely nuts about Rosie.

The two squirrels come across another wishing well. Mr. Peanuts isn't sure what to wish for this time. Now that he's met Rosie, he *has* someone special. Then he gets an idea...

"Rosie," asks Mr. Peanuts,
"will you be my valentine?"

"Of course I will!" chirps Rosie. "I'm nuts about you!" They celebrate with a romantic candlelit dinner. Being in love makes this the best Valentine's Day ever!

## About This Book

The Secret Life of Squirrels books were inspired by the busy and inquisitive squirrels in Nancy Rose's backyard in Canada. When these squirrels became regular visitors to Nancy's bird feeders, she began taking photographs of them and eventually added miniature handmade sets for fun. She creates the sets, positions them on her deck, and watches through the glass door for the squirrels' approach. Her camera is on a tripod by the door so that she can capture the squirrels in action. She makes many of her own props, such as the wishing wells, swing sets, bookshelves, park benches, furniture, and more. These days, Nancy's friends, old and new, offer her little things to use in her sets, like the tiny shopping cart.

Amazingly, she does not manipulate the photographs digitally to position the squirrels in the scenes — she gets the squirrels to pose by hiding peanuts in and around the props. Nancy enjoys photographing squirrels in particular because she loves their curiosity. It's also challenging to photograph them — they move very quickly! Sometimes it can take more than a hundred shots to get just the right image!

This book was edited by Megan Tingley and Kheryn Callender
and designed by Kristina Iulo with art direction from Saho Fujii and Jen Keenan.
The text was set in Berliner, and the display type is Woodrow.
The photographs in this book, including the squirrels and the textured backgrounds,
were taken using either a Canon 60D or Canon 6D, with various lenses, such as
the Canon 70-200mm, Canon 85mm, and Canon 100mm macro.

ISBN 978-1-338-16975-1

12 11 10 9 8 7 6 5 4 3 2 1                    18 19 20 21 22 23

Printed in the U.S.A.                    40

First Scholastic printing, January 2018